MACMILLAN READERS

PRE-INTERMEDIATE LEVEL

STEPHEN COLBOURN

Robin Hood

PRE-INTERMEDIATE LEVEL

Founding Editor: John Milne

The Macmillan Readers provide a choice of enjoyable reading materials for learners of English. The series is published at six levels – Starter, Beginner, Elementary, Pre-intermediate, Intermediate and Upper.

Level control
Information, structure and vocabulary are controlled to suit the students' ability at each level.

The number of words at each level:

Starter	about 300 basic words
Beginner	about 600 basic words
Elementary	about1100 basic words
Pre-intermediate	about 1400 basic words
Intermediate	about 1600 basic words
Upper	about 2200 basic words

Vocabulary
Some difficult words and phrases in this book are important for understanding the story. Some of these words are explained in the story and some are shown in the pictures. From Pre-intermediate level upwards, words are marked with a number like this: …³. These words are explained in the Glossary at the end of the book.

Answer keys
Answer keys for the *Points for Understanding* and the *Exercises* sections can be found at www.macmillanenglish.com

Contents

A Note About This Story

The stories of Robin Hood are very old. They are 'folk stories' – stories which people have told to each other over the last 800 years. Children heard the stories from their parents and then they told them to their own children.

Slowly, over the centuries, tales about Robin Hood – the forest outlaw[1] – were collected and written down. They were turned into songs and poetry, and more recently into plays, television dramas and films.

Robin Hood was not a 'real' person, but there are many other real people from history in the stories. King Henry II, King Richard and the Sheriff[2] of Nottingham, were real people. Sherwood Forest is a real forest.

Robin Hood came from a town called Locksley near Nottingham. He was born between the years 1160 and 1170 in the time of King Henry II. At this time, the kings of England were not English – they came from Normandy in northern France. The Normans had invaded[3] England in 1066. For two and a half centuries, the kings of England did not speak English, they spoke Norman French.

King Henry II owned more land in France than he owned in England. He fought many wars because he wanted to be King of France as well as King of England. King Henry needed money and soldiers for his wars. He raised the money by making the common[4] people of England pay very high taxes.

The Normans made laws for the Normans. These laws were very unfair. The Normans did not care about the English, so English people had no rights. English people had to work on farms that belonged to the Normans. They had to grow food and look after animals for the Normans.

There were many great forests in England where the King liked to hunt deer[5]. English people were not allowed to hunt deer, cut trees, or live in the royal forests.

If an Englishman took firewood from the forest, his ears were cut off. If an Englishman hunted small animals in the forest, his fingers were cut off. If he hunted deer, he was blinded or hanged.

For ordinary English people, the Norman barons[6] and churchmen were the same as thieves and robbers. Robin Hood was a hero to ordinary English people because he did not care about the King's laws. Robin Hood hunted the King's deer and robbed the King's men. Then he gave the money to poor and needy people.

When King Henry died, his eldest son Richard became King of England. But Richard did not spend much time in England. He went to Palestine to fight against Saladin, who was leader of the Muslim armies. Richard wanted to capture the city of Jerusalem, but he failed to do this.

While Richard was in Palestine, his mother, Queen Eleanor, and his Brother, Prince John, ruled England. Prince John became King John after Richard's death.

Archery

Robin Hood was the most famous archer[7] in England. He could shoot arrows from his bow faster and farther than anyone else.

Young men in England practised fighting and shooting every week. This was the law because the King needed archers for his wars. He offered prizes to the best archers. Every town had a special place for archery practice. Young men also practised fighting with long poles called quarter-staffs.

By law, only Normans could carry swords. Robin Hood's weapons – the bow and arrow and the quarter-staff – were the weapons of common Englishmen. However, some of the outlaws in these stories, including Robin Hood, carried swords because they lived outside the law.

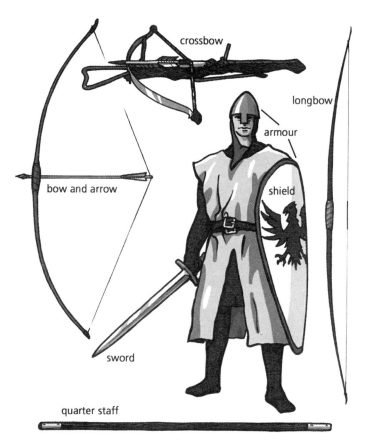

crossbow

longbow

armour

bow and arrow

shield

sword

quarter staff

The People in This Story

Robin Hood

Robin's father

Maid Marian

Friar Tuck

Much the
Miller's son

Will Stutely

Will Scarlett

Fair Ellen

Allan a Dale

Little John

Prince John

The Sheriff of
Nottingham

Sir Guy of
Gisbourne

A forester – cousin
of the sheriff

Abbot of
St Mary's

Sir Stephen

Bishop of
Hereford

Sir Richard
of Lea

King Richard

1

Robin of Locksley

Robin Hood was born in the small town of Locksley in Nottinghamshire. Locksley's buildings were made of wood and it was smoky and dirty, like many other towns in England.

Robin's father owned a small farm which didn't have very much land. Life was sometimes very hard.

The family hadn't always been poor. Robin's grandfather had been a knight[8] and he had owned a lot of land around Locksley. But then the Sheriff of Nottingham had taken the land because Robin's grandfather could not afford to pay the Sheriff's high taxes.

Robin worked on his father's farm every day. He had grown up to be tall and strong. He was fair-haired and very handsome.

Robin liked to practise archery on his father's farm, and he had become a very good archer. Many people came to watch Robin shooting his longbow. One of these people was the daughter of a local knight. Her name was Maid Marian. Marian had long blonde hair and she was very beautiful.

Robin and Marian often looked at each other. Then they began to meet secretly, and slowly they fell in love.

At this time, the King needed archers for his army. He had ordered all the strong young men in England to practise archery.

Every year, there were special archery contests[9] in England. In the small towns, the prizes were of meat and drink. In the large towns, the best archers won prize money.

One of the biggest archery contests was held in Nottingham. Every year, the Sheriff of Nottingham gave the winning archer a prize from the King. The prize – one hundred golden crowns[10] – was a lot of money. Archers came from all over England to compete[11] in the contest.

When Robin reached his eighteenth birthday, he decided to speak to his father about the contest in Nottingham.

'Father, please let me go to Nottingham,' Robin said. 'I am old enough to enter the contest and I am the best archer in Locksley. I can hit a target[12] at five hundred paces[13]. Let me compete with the archers in Nottingham. I am sure that I can win.'

His father was silent for a moment, then he replied,

'You are a very good archer, my boy. But the King and the Sheriff want archers for their wars. Don't go Robin. Stay in Locksley and be a farmer. It's not a bad life.'

'But I want to see the world,' said Robin. 'I have never been to Nottingham. And I may win one hundred golden crowns. With that money we can buy more land. And . . . then I can ask Marian to marry me!'

'You may win the contest,' replied Robin's father, 'but Marian's family still won't let you marry her. They want their daughter to marry a knight, not a farmer.'

'But your father was a knight,' said Robin. 'He owned land in Huntingdon and around Locksley.'

'That was over twenty years ago,' said his father. 'The Sheriff took most of our land when my father could not pay his taxes. Now we are poor and no one can take any more from us.'

'We are poor but honest,' replied Robin. 'I am sure that Marian will marry me for love.'

'Do not talk of love and honesty!' said his father angrily.

Robin and Marian often looked at each other.

'There is no love or honesty in England. The rich become richer while the poor become poorer. The rich make the laws, the poor pay taxes.'

But Robin was determined to go to the contest.

'Father, I *must* go to Nottingham,' Robin said. 'I am sure that I will win the Sheriff's money. Perhaps Marian will not marry me, but at least we will not be poor anymore.'

'Then go!' replied his father. 'You have seen little of the world and I pray that you return safely. Go with God and may He protect you. But go straight there and come straight back again. Do not stop on the way.'

2

How Robin Hood Became an Outlaw

Robin set off on foot for Nottingham with his longbow and arrows. It was a fine morning in June. The fields were green and the sky was blue. Robin was young and strong and he felt that the world was new. He sang as he walked along the road.

Soon he entered Sherwood Forest. Sherwood was a very large and old forest. It was full of great oak trees and the sun shone through the leaves and branches onto the road.

Robin knew that there were guards in the forest – they were called foresters. The foresters looked after the trees and the deer for the Sheriff of Nottingham and the King. No man could cut wood or shoot deer in Sherwood.

After a while, Robin came to a clearing[14]. In the clearing were fifteen men. They were eating a huge meat pie and drinking ale[15] from a tall barrel.

These men were the Sheriff's foresters. Robin knew this because the men were wearing green shirts. The colour of the shirts was called 'Lincoln green'.

The men looked up when they heard Robin.

'Where are you going, boy?' one of the foresters called. He was a large man and seemed to be the leader of the group. His mouth was full of meat pie as he spoke.

'I am going to Nottingham,' Robin answered. 'I am going to compete in the archery contest.'

The forester poured himself another cup of ale. 'Ha, ha, ha,' he laughed. 'Now boys want to enter the archery contest.

And what will you shoot with, little boy – a cheap bow and some old arrows? The contest at Nottingham is for real men with real bows and arrows.'

'My bow is as good as yours,' replied Robin angrily, 'and I can shoot farther and straighter than you.'

'Can you, my boy?' said the forester. 'Can you shoot one of those deer over there?'

The forester pointed to a herd of deer. It was very hard to see the animals because they were about five hundred paces away and partly hidden in the trees.

'Yes, I can,' answered Robin. Then he took his bow from his back and put it against his foot. He bent the bow and fixed the string to it. Then he took an arrow and put it to the bow.

'Those deer are too far away,' said the forester to the other men in the clearing. 'I'm sure that they are safe. The boy will miss, then we will kick him on his way to Nottingham!'

The other foresters laughed and drank more ale.

Robin pulled back on his bow and took careful aim[16]. Then he released the arrow and his bow sang as it flew towards the deer.

The largest of the deer jumped up then fell to the ground. The arrow had gone into the deer's neck.

'He has killed one of the King's deer!' cried one of the foresters.

'You will be punished for this!' the leader shouted at Robin. 'The Sheriff of Nottingham is my cousin and I will take you to him. He will cut off your ears and your fingers. You will never shoot a bow again.'

'Let me pass!' cried Robin. Then he ran into the trees. He ran as fast as he could and he did not look back.

The foresters had drunk too much ale and eaten too much

meat pie. They could not run fast enough to catch Robin.

'I will stop him,' said their leader. He took his bow and put an arrow to it. The forester shot the arrow at Robin's back, but his aim was bad. The arrow flew past Robin's ear and hit a tree.

Robin turned around angrily. Before the forester could shoot again, Robin put an arrow to his bow and aimed it. He let the arrow go and it flew through the air and hit the forester in the chest. Bright red blood ran down the man's Lincoln green shirt. The man cried out and fell down.

Robin turned and disappeared into the forest.

15

The foresters brought the dead man's body to Nottingham. Then they went to the Sheriff of Nottingham and told him what had happened. As he listened, the Sheriff's face turned dark with anger.

'How did this happen?' he shouted. 'You must catch the murderer who killed my cousin. Hang him!'

So the foresters travelled to all the towns on the far side of Sherwood Forest. 'Who is the young man who can shoot a deer at five hundred paces?' they asked the townspeople.

The people of Locksley knew that there was only one young man who could shoot a deer at five hundred paces. Soon the Sheriff heard the name of Robin Hood.

'I will give one hundred golden crowns to the man who brings me Robin Hood,' he said to his men. 'He has killed one of the King's foresters and one of the King's deer. He is an outlaw. Bring me Robin Hood of Locksley – dead or alive!'

3

The Outlaws of Sherwood Forest

Robin ran through the forest until he could run no more. 'I wish that forester had never spoken to me,' he thought to himself. 'I wish that I had followed a different path through the forest.'

But what was done was done. Robin was now an outlaw. He could not return to his home. He could not see his father or Maid Marian again. Now he would have to hide in the forest and live like an animal.

Robin soon realized[17] that he was not alone in the forest. Other men lived there too. The first person Robin met was called Will Stutely. Will Stutely was a thin man with sharp eyes.

'I am a barber[18],' Will Stutely explained to Robin. 'I used to shave the beards of Norman knights. Then one day I cut a man's throat and he died. Now I am a wanted man.'

Soon many other men joined them. Some of the men were in the forest because they had not paid their taxes. Some of the men had killed the King's deer in winter because there had been no food for their families. All these men were outlaws. They had come to Sherwood Forest to escape the King's soldiers.

It was easy for the outlaws to hide. Sherwood was a large forest and it was summer – the days were long and warm. There were many deer to hunt and fish to catch in the rivers. There was dry wood for making fires and nuts and berries to eat from the trees and bushes. There was wild corn in the clearings at the forest's edge.

There were now more than fifty outlaws, and that number grew each week. The outlaws wore coats of Lincoln green which they had stolen from the King's foresters. The green coats helped them to hide in the forest.

'Every day, the Sheriff robs the ordinary people with high taxes,' Robin said to the other outlaws. 'We should rob the Sheriff in return. But we will not rob him because we want to be rich. We will rob the rich to give to the poor. We will not harm women, children, or honest men. We will right wrongs when we can and we will bring hope to the people. We will live outside the law because the law is only for rich men. We will fight these rich men's unfair laws.'

———

Every day, Robin and the outlaws moved to a different part of Sherwood. They knew that the Sheriff's men often came through the forest looking for them. The Sheriff's men wanted the reward of one hundred golden crowns for Robin Hood, caught dead or alive.

'We cannot go on living like this,' Robin said to the other outlaws. 'We cannot keep running away from the Sheriff's men. We have to stop and fight.'

'But we cannot fight,' said Will Stutely. 'We only have a few bows and knives and quarter-staffs. The Sheriff's men have swords and shields[19]. They have crossbows. And there are too many of them for us to fight.'

'We will not fight them all at the same time,' replied Robin, 'but we can fight a few of them at a time. We must find somewhere where we can live without the Sheriff's men finding us. In a few weeks, it will be autumn and the leaves of the forest will turn brown and fall. The days will grow short and cold. Soon, we will need food for the winter. We must fight the winter *and* the Sheriff of Nottingham.'

So the outlaws went out in small groups. They went to explore the deepest parts of the forest. They were looking for a place where no one would be able to find them.

Robin searched the forest alone. He followed paths and crossed rivers. At last he came to a part of the wood where the sun did not shine. Here the trees and bushes grew high and thick, like a dark green wall.

Robin followed the wall until he found a narrow path which went into the deep bushes. Robin followed this path for many minutes, until he came to a clearing.

The clearing was neither damp nor dark – it was a place of light and air. It was on a high slope[20] that rose above the trees. Around the edges of the clearing was a large ring of stones. A dead oak tree with broken branches stood on the top of the slope.

Robin walked up to it. There was a crack in the side of the tree and inside was a hollow space. Robin could see something shining inside the crack. He put his hand inside and pulled out a horn[21]. The horn was made of bone and white metal. It was a hunting horn.

Robin put the horn to his lips and blew it hard.

Suddenly the trees and bushes all bent down, as if they were under a great wind. The clearing became very bright. The sound of the horn sang through the forest as Robin called the other outlaws to him. He blew the horn again and again.

The men had travelled far across Sherwood Forest but they all heard the sound of the horn. Immediately they stopped searching and followed the noise until they came to the clearing and the old oak tree.

Robin and the outlaws had found their new home.

4

Little John

The men made a simple camp in the clearing. The narrow path was the only way into the camp and it was easy to guard.

'Tomorrow we will go hunting again,' said Robin to the men. 'But this time we will go hunting for news. We need information about the Sheriff's men. We need to know who is travelling to Nottingham. Look for groups of knights. Look for tax collectors. They will travel slowly and will have money and weapons. We will welcome them here in the woods.'

––––––––

The next day, Robin went alone to the edge of Sherwood Forest. He walked along a path until he came to a river. A branch of wood crossed the river, like a bridge. Only one man could walk across this branch at a time.

A stranger was coming along the path from the opposite direction. The stranger and Robin stood at either end of the bridge. Both men carried quarter-staffs. The stranger was very tall and very broad[22]. He was the biggest man that Robin had ever seen.

'Let the better man cross first,' shouted the stranger to Robin. The stranger had a handsome, happy face. He smiled at Robin as he spoke.

Robin also smiled.

'Then let me pass,' he said, 'for I am the better man.'

'Ah! We shall see,' said the stranger. Then he lifted his quarter-staff in both hands. He was ready to fight.

Robin took hold of his own quarter-staff and stepped onto the branch. The stranger also stepped onto the branch and the two men began to fight.

Robin was tall but the stranger was taller. Robin was broad but the stranger was broader. Both men were strong. They moved backwards and forwards along the narrow branch as they fought.

After many minutes of fighting, the stranger hit Robin hard on the side of his head. Robin fell into the water and the stranger laughed.

'Now, who is the better man?' said the man. 'Here, give me your hand. You have given me good exercise today.'

He helped Robin out of the water and the two men sat next to the river.

'What is your name?' asked Robin.

'I am called John Little,' said the stranger.

'Have you ever heard of Robin Hood?' asked Robin.

'Of course I have,' said John Little. 'He is an outlaw who lives here in the forest. The Sheriff of Nottingham is looking for him. But I have no love for the Sheriff and his men, so I hope that he doesn't catch Robin Hood.'

'Would you like to join Robin Hood and his group of outlaws?' asked Robin.

John Little looked at Robin carefully. 'Who are you?' he asked. 'Why do you want me to become an outlaw?'

Robin did not answer. Instead, he took his horn from his belt and blew it three times. Soon his men came running from the forest. They came to the river and stood around Robin and John Little.

'My name is Robin Hood and these are my men,' Robin said. 'Will you join us?'

'I see many men around you,' said John Little. 'But I still

*Both men were strong. They moved backwards and forwards
along the narrow branch as they fought.*

do not know you – I only know the name Robin Hood. I also know that Robin Hood is a very good archer. Show me that you can shoot an arrow and I will believe you.'

Robin lifted his bow and arrow. 'Tell me what to shoot,' he said.

John Little looked around and pointed into the forest.

'Do you see that young tree?' he asked. 'It's about five hundred paces away and no broader than a man's hand. Can you shoot an arrow into that tree?'

'It is not an easy target,' said Robin. 'You have chosen well.'

Robin put an arrow to his bow. Then he took aim and shot the arrow into the young tree.

'You *must be* Robin Hood,' said John Little. 'Well, I do not love the Sheriff, nor the men who collect taxes from the common people. So yes, Robin Hood, I will join you and your men.'

Robin smiled at the big man. Then he laughed loudly.

'We must have a feast to celebrate!' he said. 'And to welcome you to our home in Sherwood Forest.'

In the forest clearing, by the old oak tree, the outlaws built a great fire and roasted an ox[23]. They ate the ox and drank ale until they were full. At the end of the feast, Robin took a cup of ale and held it over John Little's head.

'You are the biggest man I have ever seen,' Robin said. 'And now you are one of us so we will give you a new name. We shall call you Little John.'

And Robin poured the ale over Little John's head.

5

Will Stutely the Barber

The Sheriff of Nottingham collected taxes from all the neighbouring towns. His tax collectors were knights and barons and churchmen. One of these churchmen, the Abbot[24] of St Mary's, came to Nottingham every year. The Abbot brought the taxes he had collected from the town of Doncaster. Knights and soldiers helped him guard the money as he travelled.

'Soon the Abbot of St Mary's will pass through the forest on his journey to Nottingham,' Robin told the outlaws. 'We must be ready to welcome him. Go out of the forest and look for the Abbot. Come back and tell me how many men are travelling with him.'

But the Sheriff of Nottingham was not stupid. 'Robin Hood will learn that the Abbot of St Mary's is coming to Nottingham,' he told his men. 'I am sure that he will try to steal the tax money from the Abbot as he travels through Sherwood Forest. But we must be ready for him. We will catch Robin Hood and we will hang him from a high tree.'

Will Stutely set out to look for the Abbot and his men. He decided to search the north side of the forest because he knew that the Abbot would pass that way. Will had sharp eyes and a quick mind. He also had a plan.

Will watched and waited. Soon he saw a group coming towards him. With them was the Abbot. He was riding in a covered wagon that was pulled by six white horses. There were many knights and soldiers around him.

24

The wagon moved slowly. 'There must be gold in that wagon,' thought Will Stutely. 'It is heavy – and so is the Abbot. He is very fat.'

Will followed the Abbot and his men to a small town at the edge of Sherwood Forest. Then he watched as the men stopped at a small inn. It was evening now and Will guessed that they would spend the night there.

Will Stutely was a barber. He always carried a pair of scissors and a razor[25] with him. The men who travelled with the Abbot were Normans and Normans liked to be shaved every day. They liked to have very short hair on their heads, so they often needed the services of a barber. But the Normans preferred to be shaved by Norman barbers. They did not trust every barber with a sharp razor!

Will Stutely slept by the road near the inn. In the morning, he woke to the sound of the Abbot's men. They were calling for a barber!

'Barbeur! Barbeur!' the knights called in Norman French. But there was no barber at the inn.

Will Stutely stepped forward.

'I am a barber, good sirs,' he told them. 'May I be of service to you?'

One of the knights spoke English. He looked at Will Stutely coldly. 'Do you know how to shave a monk's[26] head?' the knight asked.

'Yes, I do sir,' said Will. 'I have cut the hair of many monks at Fountains Abbey[27] and at the Abbey of . . .'

'Enough!' shouted the knight. 'Be silent! These men have decided to become monks.' He pointed at the group of knights. 'Cut their hair and shave their heads. Do it carefully and you will be paid. If you are careless, you will be whipped[28].'

25

Will Stutely started to shave the men's heads, but it was a strange task. Knights did not usually shave their heads like monks! Why did they want to do this?

As Will worked, he was listening to what the men were saying. The men spoke Norman French and they did not think that Will understood them. But Will Stutely had worked as a barber at an abbey and he knew enough Norman French to understand the men's conversation.

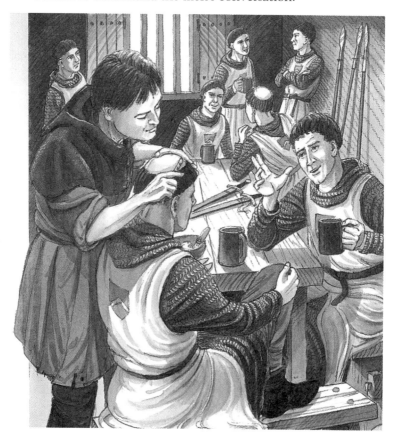

'Robin Hood and his outlaws will think we are monks because we will have shaved heads,' said one of the knights. 'He will think that we have no weapons.'

'We will surprise them all,' said another knight. 'We will catch and kill these outlaws of Sherwood Forest!'

After their hair was cut, the knights put on the clothes of monks – brown clothes that covered their swords and armour.

Will Stutely watched and listened. The large, heavy wagon was still outside the inn. But now there was also a smaller, open cart. The soldiers put bags of flour into this open cart. Then they pushed smaller, heavier bags under the bags of flour. Will guessed that these were bags of golden crowns. He counted forty bags altogether.

Then the Abbot of St Mary's came out of the inn. He sat in the smaller, open cart. He was not wearing the clothes of a churchman. He was wearing the clothes of a miller[29].

The larger, covered wagon set off along the main road. The knights, who were now dressed as monks, went with the covered wagon.

The Abbot of St Mary's travelled along another, smaller road. Two knights rode beside his cart. A group of women walked behind him. One of the women carried a small child.

The group travelled slowly. Will Stutely travelled faster. He went to tell Robin what he had seen.

6

The Abbot of St Mary's

The covered wagon moved slowly into Sherwood Forest. It was heavy and the road was full of holes. The knights watched the road in front of them carefully. They looked for outlaws in the trees.

'We are in the middle of the forest now,' said one of the knights. 'I am sure that Robin Hood and his men will attack us soon. Don't worry. The Sheriff and his men are coming from Nottingham and we will catch the outlaws when they attack us. We will kill them all.'

Suddenly an arrow flew out of the forest. It hit one of the knights in the chest. The knight was not hurt because he was wearing armour under his brown monk's clothes.

Then a tall man stepped into the road.

'Stop right there!' the tall man shouted. 'I am Robin Hood. All people passing through Sherwood Forest must pay me a tax.'

Immediately the covers of the wagon opened and men armed with crossbows jumped out. The knights pulled out their swords and one of them blew a hunting horn.

Another horn answered from farther up the road. The Sheriff's men were coming!

The tall man in the road looked surprised. 'Run! There are too many of them – we are surrounded[30]!' he shouted, but the knights could not see who he was shouting to.

'Go after him!' cried one of the knights. 'It's Robin Hood. Catch him!'

The tall man ran into the forest and the knights ran after him. The soldiers followed and so did the crossbowmen. They chased the tall man for half the day, but Little John knew the forest too well and the knights could not catch him.

Little John had been alone. The other outlaws were with the real Robin Hood – in another part of the forest.

———

Robin was standing in the middle of a narrow road when the fat miller appeared. The miller was riding in the smaller, open cart. Two knights rode on horses beside the cart. The women and child walked a little way behind.

'Where are you going, good miller?' Robin called out.

The miller did not reply. Instead, the knight who spoke English said, 'We are going to Nottingham. Let us pass. Or do you mean to hurt these women and the child?'

'I am talking to the miller,' said Robin, 'let him answer.' But the fat miller said nothing.

So Robin walked up to the cart. 'All travellers who pass through Sherwood must pay a tax,' he told the miller. 'We will take a little flour from you, but we will take only the small bags.'

The miller's face turned red. Suddenly he put his hand into his shirt and pulled out a sword, but Robin caught the miller's hand.

'This is a pretty sword,' said Robin. 'It does not belong to a miller, I am sure. I will take it as a gift from you.'

Then Robin pulled the miller out of the cart and threw him onto the road.

Suddenly, twenty outlaws stepped out of the trees. They aimed their bows and arrows at the knights. The knights and the miller were surrounded.

'I am Sir Roger of Doncaster,' said the knight who spoke English. 'Who is this outlaw who robs women and a poor miller?'

'I am Robin Hood of Sherwood Forest,' answered Robin. 'And we shall see if this miller is *really* poor.'

Then two of the outlaws climbed into the cart. They moved the large bags of flour. Underneath they found the forty bags of golden crowns.

'Tell me, how does a miller have forty bags of golden crowns?' asked Robin. 'Who is the *real* thief here?'

The miller did not answer. Instead he watched silently as the outlaws lifted the forty bags of gold from the wagon.

'Now go in peace,' said Robin. 'And give my good wishes to the Sheriff of Nottingham.'

And so the knights and the Abbot and the women went on their way to Nottingham. Robin and his men travelled back to their camp in the middle of the forest. They carried the forty bags of gold with them.

The Abbot of St Mary's was no poorer because of Robin Hood. The gold had not been his – it was tax that he had collected for the Sheriff of Nottingham. But the Abbot was still a very angry man.

'I will have my revenge,' he said to Roger of Doncaster. 'I do not care how long it takes, but I will find a way to kill Robin Hood!'

———

The Abbot of St Mary's was a rich and powerful man. He had friends at the King's court in London. These friends told the King about Robin Hood.

'Forty bags of gold!' shouted King Henry angrily. 'The Sheriff of Nottingham let an outlaw steal forty bags of gold? Send for the Sheriff. Let him explain himself!'

But when the Sheriff of Nottingham arrived to see the King, he was met by King Henry's youngest son, Prince John. King Henry had gone to France. He had left to fight a war against the French king.

Prince John was a dark-haired man. He was only twenty-one years old but he was already getting fat. John loved food and he often ate so much that he became ill.

'Good Sheriff of Nottingham,' John said, 'I hear that we have a problem. What shall we do about this outlaw called Robin Hood?'

'My lord, I shall take care of it,' said the Sheriff. 'I promise you that I will catch Robin Hood and hang him.'

'Make sure that you do,' said Prince John. 'Also, know this – that after his death, my father wishes me to become King of England. He does not want Richard to be King. And, when I am King, I will need good servants like you – the Sheriff of Nottingham.'

The Sheriff bowed[31] his head to Prince John. 'My lord, you know that I am your true servant,' he said.

'Good,' said Prince John. 'As you know, my brother Richard likes fighting. He believes in truth and justice[32]. But I think you are a man like myself, good Sheriff. We both know that the most important thing in life is money.'

7

The Golden Arrow

The Sheriff returned to Nottingham. It was harvest time[33] – time to cut and collect the corn from the fields at the end of summer. There was always a great festival after the harvest.

'This year we will have a special harvest festival,' said the Sheriff to the people of Nottingham. 'We will have an archery contest. Prince John will give a special prize. The prize will be an arrow made from gold.'

The Sheriff sent messengers to all the towns and villages. Soon news of the contest reached Robin.

'A golden arrow is a good prize,' Robin told the other outlaws. 'But I know why the Sheriff of Nottingham is having this contest. It's a trap. He is expecting me to come so that he can catch me and hang me.'

Robin was right. The Sheriff *did* expect Robin to come to the archery contest. He planned to trap Robin and his men in Nottingham town.

'Watch out for Robin Hood,' the Sheriff told his soldiers and other knights. 'He is a tall, fair man. Many of you have seen him and heard him speak. He is a brave outlaw. I am sure he will come to the archery contest. He will try to disguise[34] himself, but we will know him.'

On the day of the archery contest, the Sheriff dressed in his best clothes. He looked very handsome in his purple cloak and a velvet cap. But underneath his clothes he was wearing armour.

Archers had come from all over England for the contest.

The archery range was decorated with flags and ribbons of coloured cloth. All the people of Nottingham town came to watch the archers. The people cheered and shouted as the Sheriff stood up and raised his hand.

'All men who wish to enter the contest may shoot an arrow,' he said. 'But only the twelve best men can enter the contest.'

For the first hour, a hundred men took turns to shoot an arrow at a target. There was a black circle at the centre of the target. The black circle was called a 'bull's eye'. Some of the archers missed the target completely. Some of them hit the edge of the target. Only twelve men hit inside the bull's eye.

Among the twelve men was the Sheriff's champion archer. His name was Gilbert Red Cap. The Sheriff watched the other eleven men carefully. Some of them he knew, but half of them were strangers.

'Find out the names of the strangers,' he said to his steward[35]. 'Robin Hood will not tell us his name, but we know he is tall and fair. Can you see anyone who matches his description?'

'There is one tall, fair-haired man among these twelve archers,' replied the steward. 'I cannot see his face clearly because he wears a blue hood[36]. I will try to find out his name.'

The Sheriff stood up and the crowd became silent.

'You will all shoot three arrows in the first round[37],' the Sheriff explained to the twelve archers. 'The target is one hundred and twenty paces away. The six best archers from the first round will go into the second round. Those six archers will shoot two arrows at a target that is two hundred and forty paces away.

'The three best archers from the second round will go into the third round,' the Sheriff continued. 'In this final round, the archers will shoot one arrow each. The target will be three hundred and sixty paces away. The winner will be the man who shoots closest to the centre of the bull's eye.'

Then the Sheriff raised his hand and trumpets sounded.

'Let the first round begin,' he cried.

The tall stranger dressed in blue stepped forward. He gave his name as William of London. All three of his arrows hit the bull's eye. The crowd cheered.

The other archers took turns to shoot. The next archer did not hit the target and the archer after him hit it only once.

The next two archers hit the bull's eye with their three arrows. Then Gilbert Red Cap stepped forward. He shot his three arrows quickly. They all hit near to the centre of the bull's eye.

'Hurrah Gilbert!' shouted the crowd.

The last archer to shoot in the contest was a strange man. His back was bent and he was dressed like a beggar – a very poor man. His clothes were made of many pieces of red cloth. His hair and beard were brown and he had only one eye. A black patch covered half his face and his right eye.

'He is a strange-looking man,' said the Sheriff to the steward. 'What is his name?'

'He calls himself Jack of Lincoln,' replied the steward. 'He was hurt in the King's wars.'

'I am sure that he cannot shoot straight with only one eye and a bent back,' said the Sheriff.

The beggar stepped forward. The crowd shouted and laughed at the beggar's strange clothes and his bent back.

The beggar did not look at the crowd. He drew back his bow and aimed an arrow at the target. He shot the arrow and hit the centre of the bull's eye. Then he quickly shot two more arrows into the bull's eye.

The crowd was silent. 'That beggar is lucky,' said the Sheriff. 'But he will not beat Gilbert. Move the targets back to two hundred and forty paces!'

The six best archers from the first round shot again. This time they shot two arrows each. William of London shot well. Both his arrows hit the bull's eye. The next two archers were not so lucky. Gilbert Red Cap shot close to the very centre of the bull's eye. The strange beggar also shot both his arrows into the bull's eye.

'There are only three men left,' said the Sheriff to his steward. 'That beggar is a good archer. But the man to watch is William of London. Tell the soldiers to stand near him. I'm sure he is Robin Hood. He won't escape me this time.'

Then the Sheriff stood up.

'Move the targets back to three hundred and sixty paces!' he shouted.

The crowd went silent as William of London stepped forward and pulled back the blue hood of his cloak. He was tall and fair – just like the description of Robin Hood!

William took careful aim. He shot an arrow and hit the bull's eye, but he did not hit very near to its centre.

'A good shot,' said the Sheriff, 'but Gilbert can do better. Hurrah for Gilbert!'

'Hurrah for Gilbert!' shouted the crowd.

Then Gilbert stepped forward. He drew back his bow and took careful aim. The arrow hit the centre of the bull's eye.

The crowd went wild. 'Gilbert! Gilbert!' they shouted.

'He has won,' said the Sheriff. 'My champion archer has won. He is better than Robin Hood.'

When the beggar stepped forward to take his shot, the crowd were not watching him. They were talking excitedly about Gilbert.

Slowly, the beggar drew back his bow. Then he took careful aim with his one good eye and shot his arrow.

Suddenly the crowd stopped talking. Something strange had happened. Everyone was looking at the target.

Then a knight came towards the Sheriff.

'Gilbert's arrow is broken, my lord,' he said. 'The stranger's arrow has split Gilbert's arrow. It has gone right through to the very centre of the bull's eye.'

The crowd had gone very quiet. The Sheriff was not pleased, but he tried to smile. He raised the prize in his hand and showed it to the crowd. It was an arrow made of pure gold – a golden arrow.

'Come forward,' said the Sheriff to the beggar. 'I need good archers and I invite you to join my army. You can eat my meat, drink my ale and live under my roof. What do you say about that?'

The beggar stood up straight and looked at the Sheriff.

'I say no, sir,' he said. 'For I am my own man. I have no need of a lord and master.'

Then the beggar took the golden arrow from the Sheriff and held it up to show the crowd. The people cheered.

'You are a very rude beggar,' said the Sheriff. 'Get out of Nottingham now, or you will be whipped for your rudeness.'

The beggar turned and disappeared into the crowd. He held the golden arrow high above his head.

The Sheriff was so angry that he forgot about Robin Hood. He called for his horse and rode quickly back to the castle.

That evening, the Sheriff ate a great meal with his favourite knights.

'I expected Robin Hood to come to the contest,' he told the knights, 'but he is not brave enough to show his face in Nottingham.'

Suddenly, there was a noise. An arrow had hit the castle's wooden ceiling.

'Where did that arrow come from?' asked the Sheriff.

'It came through the window, my lord,' answered his steward. 'There is a piece of paper tied to it.'

'Quick, give the paper to me!' said the Sheriff. He tore the paper from the arrow. It was a message.

38

> We eat and drink in Sherwood, for today
> The Sheriff gave a golden prize away.
>
> Robin Hood — the beggar

The Sheriff's face turned red and he ate no more that night, but the outlaws in Sherwood Forest shared a great feast.

Robin washed the brown colour from his hair and beard and took off the eye patch. He lifted the bag of flour from under the back of his shirt.

Then he hung the arrow on the old oak tree. It was his prize for everyone to see. It was his prize for being the best archer in England.

8

The Rescue of Will Stutely

For seven days and seven nights, Robin and his men stayed in Sherwood Forest. They hid in the clearing and did not show themselves to anyone.

'We must choose where and when we will fight the Sheriff's men,' said Robin. 'I do not want to lose a single man in an unequal fight against knights, soldiers and crossbowmen.'

But the outlaws heard no news of the Sheriff or his men. For a whole week things stayed quiet. Robin became worried. He wanted to know what the Sheriff was doing.

At the end of the week, Robin thought of a plan. He called Will Stutely.

'Go in disguise to the Blue Boar Inn on the far side of the forest,' he said. 'Speak to the landlord there. He's our friend. Find out what the Sheriff is doing.'

So Will Stutely put on monk's clothing and went to the Blue Boar Inn. He carried a sword underneath his clothes.

When Will reached the inn, he sat down at the table and waited to speak to the landlord.

Soon a group of the Sheriff's men arrived. There were many travellers at the inn. The Sheriff's men wanted to look at the travellers and ask them questions about Robin Hood.

When Will Stutely saw the Sheriff's men enter the inn, he stood up and went to pray in a quiet corner of the room. He knelt down on the ground. Then he pulled his brown hood down over his face so that no one would recognize him.

The Sheriff's men went around the inn. They looked at

everyone and asked questions. But they did not speak to the monk in the corner of the room.

The Blue Boar Inn had many cats. Suddenly, a large cat rubbed against Will Stutely's knee. The cat raised the brown cloth of Will's monk clothes and showed the Lincoln green beneath!

'Look!' said one of the Sheriff's men, 'he is not a monk! He is wearing Lincoln green. He is one of Robin Hood's men!'

The soldier pulled out his sword. Immediately, Will Stutely stood up and pulled out his own sword. But there were too many of the Sheriff's men to fight. Will Stutely cut one man with his sword before he was pulled down to the floor. Then his hands and feet were tied with ropes and he was taken to Nottingham.

———

Immediately, the landlord of the Blue Boar Inn sent a messenger into Sherwood Forest. The messenger carried a note for Robin.

WILL STUTELY HAS BEEN TAKEN PRISONER BY THE SHERIFF OF NOTTINGHAM. HE WILL BE HANGED TOMORROW OUTSIDE NOTTINGHAM TOWN.

Robin was shocked and angry when he read the message. He knew that he and the outlaws had to help Will Stutely.

'We have to help Will,' Robin told them. 'But there are so many of the Sheriff's men. It will be very dangerous and we must disguise ourselves as ordinary men. But we must try to save Will or he will be hanged tomorrow.'

So Robin and the outlaws travelled to the edge of the forest. They asked for news from passing travellers. They waited and watched.

Then Robin made a decision. 'I think we should go into Nottingham in small groups,' he said. 'We can join the crowd. We need to be close to Will when they bring him out from the castle.'

So the group of outlaws travelled into the town in ones and twos. They stood near the castle and waited for Will to be brought out.

The sun was low in the sky when the castle gates finally opened and some soldiers appeared. The men were guarding an open cart. In the middle of the cart stood Will Stutely. His face was pale and a rope was tied around his neck and his hands.

Will Stutely turned to the Sheriff of Nottingham, who was riding a horse next to the cart.

'Give me a sword!' Will shouted, 'so that I can fight you and all your men.'

But the Sheriff only laughed at Will. Then he turned and spoke to one of his men.

'This man is an outlaw and a thief and a murderer,' he said. 'We will hang him outside the town gates. Let this be a warning to Robin Hood and the outlaws of Sherwood Forest.'

As Will and the Sheriff arrived at the town gates, the crowd started to press hard around the cart.

'Push these people away!' said the Sheriff to his men. 'Get away!' he shouted at the crowd.

Then a large man pushed his way to the cart. It was Little John. He climbed onto the cart and cut the rope that was tied around Will Stutely's hands. The soldiers could not move because there were too many people around them. Their arms were pressed to their sides.

'Get back! Get back!' shouted the Sheriff. He pulled out his sword, but he was too close to the cart. Little John took hold of the Sheriff's arm and pulled the sword from his hand.

Suddenly there were outlaws all around the cart. Arrows flew and the crowd ran in all directions. One of the soldiers cried out and fell down. Then the outlaws aimed their arrows at the Sheriff.

'Back! Back!' shouted the Sheriff. He was suddenly very afraid. He turned his horse and rode back through the gates of the town. His men followed him quickly.

The road to Sherwood Forest was clear – there were no more soldiers or knights. Robin led Will Stutely and the outlaws back to the clearing.

'We may not be so lucky next time,' Robin told the outlaws. 'Let's stay in the forest and prepare for winter. I'm sure that the Sheriff will not trouble us again until spring time.'

And so the outlaws collected food and prepared their camp for winter. They kept themselves warm through the long dark days and waited patiently for spring to arrive.

9

Will Scarlett

It was six months later and Robin and Little John were walking through the forest on a bright spring day. The sun was shining through the leaves and there were many bright flowers growing in the grass.

'Who's that strangely-dressed man?' Little John asked suddenly. 'His clothes are very bright.'

Robin looked ahead and saw a young man walking along the road towards them. The man's clothes were bright red and he held a red rose in his hand. His hair was long and yellow.

'He looks like a baron's son,' said Little John. 'He's carrying a sword. Is he also carrying a heavy purse, I wonder?'

Robin and Little John waited until the stranger was about to pass. Then Robin stepped in front of the man and said,

'Stop, sir! You walk through Sherwood Forest. Do you know there is a tax to pay?'

'Why should I stop?' asked the stranger, 'and why should I pay you a tax?'

'It is the law of Sherwood Forest' said Robin. 'First show us your purse. Then we will let you pass.'

'I can show you my purse, but it has no money in it,' said the stranger. 'Now, let me pass or I will fight you.' Then the man pulled out his sword.

Robin and Little John laughed.

'We do not want to hurt you,' said Robin. 'We are two strong men. You have a sword. We have quarter-staffs. Will this be an equal fight?'

44

'Then let's make it an equal fight,' said the stranger. 'I will fight one of you with a quarter-staff. If I win, you will let me pass. If I lose, you will take my purse – though it has no money in it.'

'Very well,' said Robin. 'Little John can lend you his quarter-staff. Then I will fight you.'

Little John handed his quarter-staff to the stranger.

The stranger put down his sword and immediately attacked Robin with the quarter-staff.

Robin was surprised. The stranger had broad shoulders and strong arms. He was a very good fighter. Robin was trying hard to defend himself. This was not an easy fight.

'You fight well,' said Robin after some minutes. 'You hit quickly. Where did you learn to use the quarter-staff?'

'I fight, I don't talk,' said the stranger. Then he aimed his quarter-staff at Robin's head. Robin lifted his own quarter-staff in both hands. The stranger hit down hard and Robin's quarter-staff broke into two pieces.

45

'Wait!' Robin cried. 'You win, good sir. Now, tell us your name and where you are going.'

'My name is Will Gamwell,' said the young man, 'and I am looking for Robin Hood.'

'Why do you want to find Robin Hood?' asked Robin.

'I had a disagreement with my father's steward,' said Will Gamwell. 'Now I need Robin Hood's help.'

'And why do you want Robin Hood to help you?' asked Little John.

'Because I got angry and broke the steward's neck. I killed him,' said Will Gamwell. 'Now the Sheriff of Nottingham is looking for me. So I have become an outlaw. That's why I want to join Robin Hood and his men in Sherwood Forest.'

'Then welcome,' said Robin. 'I am Robin Hood and Sherwood Forest needs good strong men like you.'

So Robin and Little John took Will Gamwell into Sherwood Forest and showed him to their camp. They gave him the name Will Scarlett – because of his bright red clothes.

10

Much the Miller's Son

A few days later, Robin went out hunting with Little John and Will Scarlett. Late in the afternoon, they saw a young miller walking towards them. The miller was carrying a sack of flour on his back. He was covered with white dust.

'That is Much the Miller's Son,' said Will Scarlett. 'His father was hanged for hunting the King's deer. Now Much has to pay extra taxes to the Sheriff of Nottingham. He has no money and his life is very hard.'

'I think we should play a joke on Much the Miller's Son,' said Robin. 'Then we will take him into the forest and give him a good meal.'

'Wait!' Robin called to Much as he passed them. 'Your sack of flour is very heavy. We will help you carry it.'

'I can carry my own sack of flour,' replied Much.

'It's too heavy,' said Little John. 'We will take some of your flour, then your sack will be lighter.'

'You are going to rob me,' said Much. 'Do you know that you are in Robin Hood's forest? Robin Hood will not let you rob an honest man.'

'I do not fear Robin Hood any more than I fear myself,' said Robin. 'Now we want to look in your sack of flour. Please, show it to us.'

Much the Miller's Son pretended to be afraid. 'Please do not rob me, good sirs,' he said. 'I am a poor man. Look in my sack and you will see only flour.'

The miller put down the sack and opened it. Robin and the others looked inside the sack.

Suddenly Much put his hands into the sack and threw flour into the faces of the men.

For a moment, Robin and his outlaws were blinded. They put their hands to their faces and rubbed their eyes.

Then Much the Miller's Son took hold of Little John's quarter-staff. He hit Robin and the other two men with the staff.

'Thieves! Robbers!' he shouted, and he hit the three men again. 'Robin Hood will hear about this! Just you wait. Robin Hood will hear that you tried to rob an honest man.'

Then Robin and his men began to laugh loudly.

'Wait! Wait! Stop, good miller, we beg you,' said Robin. 'I am Robin Hood and these are my men.'

'You are a liar,' said Much the Miller's Son. And he hit the men again.

The three men put their hands over their heads to protect themselves. Will Scarlett's clothes had turned white with flour.

Then Robin took out his horn and blew it three times. Soon his men came running out of the forest. Much the Miller's Son looked at the outlaws in surprise. He was suddenly very afraid.

'Please, do not fear us,' said Robin. 'You are a great man. Will you join our group of outlaws and live with us in the forest?'

'If you can forgive me for hitting you,' said Much, 'then I will be happy to join you and your group. I cannot live as a miller because the Sheriff's men take my flour. How can honest men live in times like these?'

The outlaws laughed and took Much the Miller's Son into the forest. And that night they ate and drank and welcomed another man to their group.

11

Allan a Dale

That summer, King Henry died, and Richard became King of England. But Richard did not stay in England for long. He went to Palestine to fight and soon more taxes were needed to pay for this new war.

The Sheriff and his men were busy. They collected taxes from everyone. They collected taxes in the name of Richard's brother, Prince John. While Richard was away, Prince John was the ruler of England.

Meanwhile, little had changed in the forest except that the old oak tree grew new green leaves. The dead tree had come back to life.

On the first day of that spring and on Midsummer's day, a white lady was seen in the forest. From then on, the White Lady of the Woods always sang at each change of season. No man knew who she was or where she had come from.

———

One day, towards evening, Will Scarlett and Will Stutely heard a man singing in the forest.

'That is a very sad song,' said Will Stutely. 'Let's see who's singing it.'

They followed the sound until they came to a clearing in the trees. There they found a young man with untidy clothes. He was playing the harp[38] and singing. He looked very unhappy and he was crying as he sang.

'I know your face,' said Will Scarlett to the man, 'and I know your voice. You are a minstrel[39]. You sang at my father's house not long ago. Why are you so sad?'

'Because my true love has been taken from me,' replied the minstrel. 'Her name is Fair Ellen. Ellen and I want to get married. But Ellen's father will not allow her to marry me because I am a poor minstrel. Ellen's father is a poor farmer. He wants her to marry an old knight called Sir Stephen. Ellen's father owes money to Sir Stephen.'

'And what is your name?' asked Will Stutely.

'My name is Allan a Dale,' said the minstrel.

'Then come with us, Allan a Dale,' said Will Stutely. 'You must tell your story to Robin Hood.'

And so they went to the outlaws' camp. It was evening time and the outlaws were preparing to eat supper[40].

'You are welcome to eat with us, young minstrel,' said Robin, 'but after you have eaten you must sing for your supper!'

And so Allan a Dale sang for the outlaws. He sang a very sad song about his love for Fair Ellen. He sang about how Fair Ellen had to marry an old man who she did not love.

Even Little John was nearly crying. 'Please stay with us, Allan a Dale,' he said. 'You sing very beautifully and we have need of good company. Stay with us and you can sing like a bird every day.'

'Thank you,' said Allan a Dale, 'but I cannot stay. I am too unhappy because my Fair Ellen is a prisoner in her father's house. She will be married to Sir Stephen the day after tomorrow. They will marry at the church in Rotherdale.'

'Then we must try to help you,' said Robin. 'Stay with us tonight. In the morning we will make plans.'

As Robin spoke, he was thinking sadly about Maid Marian, his own lost love. Would he ever see her again?

So Allan a Dale stayed with the outlaws that night. He sang and told stories of King Arthur and his knights in the old days. All the outlaws listened in silence. Then they fell into restful sleep.

12

Friar⁴¹ Tuck

'I know of a monk who can help Allan a Dale to marry Ellen,' Will Scarlett told Robin the next day. 'He is called the Friar of Fountain Dale. He lives on the edge of the forest beside a river. Although he is a friar, he is also a good fighter.'

'Then let's go and find this strange friar,' said Robin.

So Robin went with Little John and Will Scarlett to find Fountain Dale. After a few hours, the road came to a river. On the side of the river sat a large man who wore the grey clothes of a friar. The top of his head was bald and he had a thick neck, like a bull. His face was red and happy. He was eating a meat pie and drinking wine from a leather bottle. In between mouthfuls of food, the friar talked to himself and sang songs.

'I will speak to this happy friar,' said Robin to Little John and Will Scarlett. 'Wait here in the trees and watch. Come only if I blow my horn.'

So Will Scarlett and Little John hid in the trees. They watched as Robin walked up to the friar.

'Good day, master friar,' Robin said. 'Can you show me the way to Fountain Dale?'

The friar looked up at Robin. Then he put his hand on a sword that lay beside him.

'A friar who carries a sword?' said Robin in surprise. 'This is very strange.'

'I am a fighting friar,' said the big man. 'The roads are not safe these days and there are many outlaws in the forest.'

'I have heard of these dangerous outlaws,' said Robin.

'Now, can you tell me the way to Fountain Dale?'

'Yes, I can,' said the friar. 'If you carry me across the river, I will show you where it is.'

'Carry you?' said Robin in surprise.

'I will ride on your back,' said the friar. 'The river is deep and I want to keep my clothes dry. If you give me your sword and your bow, I will hold them and keep them dry for you.'

So Robin lifted the friar onto his back. The man was very heavy and they crossed the river slowly. The friar held the sword and bow tightly in his hand.

The friar's clothes were dry when they reached the other side of the river, but Robin's were very wet.

'Now, good friar, where is Fountain Dale?' asked Robin.

'It's over there,' said the friar. And he pointed back to the other side of the river.

'Over there?' asked Robin. 'But we have just come from there. Why didn't you tell me when we were on that side of the river?'

'I promised to *show* you the way,' said the friar. 'I could not see it from over there so I could not show you. Now you can see the way, so please carry me back across the river. Then I will return your sword and bow and we can both continue on our journeys.'

Robin was angry now. He was wet and the friar was heavy. But the friar was also holding Robin's sword and bow. Slowly, Robin lifted the friar onto his back. The man felt even heavier than before.

They started to cross the river again. Robin was a strong man but the friar was heavier than two sacks of flour. The river was deep and Robin could not see where to put his feet. In the middle of the river, Robin slipped and fell. Both men sank into the water and the friar let go of the sword and bow.

It was the friar's turn to be angry now, but Robin was laughing as the two men climbed out of the river.

'I will teach you not to laugh at a fighting friar,' the friar shouted at Robin. 'I will fight you. I will do terrible things to you!'

'Wait, master friar,' said Robin, laughing loudly. 'My name is Robin Hood and I have many friends in the forest who will help me. I will call them.'

Then Robin took the horn from his belt and blew it.

Little John and Will Scarlett ran out of the forest and

joined Robin. The friar looked closely at Will Scarlett.

'I know you,' the friar said. 'You are William Gamwell. What are you doing here?'

'We have come to invite you to Sherwood Forest,' said Will Scarlett. Then he turned to Robin. 'This man is Friar Tuck,' he said. 'He is a very good fighter. He also loves his food.'

'Well, we have plenty of food and drink in Sherwood Forest,' said Robin. 'Will you come and eat with us, Friar Tuck?'

Friar Tuck smiled. 'I am always ready to eat and fight,' he said, 'but now is not the time for fighting.'

'I will always remember our meeting, Friar Tuck,' replied Robin, 'and how I carried you across the river like a horse carries a rider!'

'My body is heavy but my heart is light,' said Friar Tuck. 'Come, let's eat and drink and be merry. I feel hungry again already!'

And so they went into the forest and ate a great meal. Friar Tuck was the latest man to join Robin Hood and his outlaws in Sherwood Forest.

13

Fair Ellen

It was the day of Fair Ellen's wedding. Ellen was going to marry Sir Stephen at the church in Rotherdale.

'Sir Stephen is an old knight,' said Allan a Dale. 'And Fair Ellen's father owes Sir Stephen two hundred crowns. Sir Stephen has promised to forget the debt if he can marry Ellen.'

'We must go to the wedding,' said Robin. 'We will go to the church at Rotherdale.'

So Robin, Little John, Allan a Dale and Friar Tuck all went to the wedding. Robin was disguised in the clothes of a minstrel. His coat was red and yellow and he wore a feather in his hat. Other outlaws followed behind the four men.

Robin and the men arrived at the village of Rotherdale and waited near the church. Soon six horsemen came along the road. One of the horsemen was Sir Stephen, the fat old knight who was going to marry Fair Ellen. Beside him rode the Bishop[42] of Hereford and four soldiers.

'Wait, my Lord Bishop!' Robin said to the group as he rode past. 'I am a minstrel. I can play music for you after the wedding.'

'Then let me hear how well you play,' replied the Bishop.

'No, my lord, I cannot do that. I will play only for the bride,' Robin told him.

'You are a very rude man,' said the Bishop. 'After the wedding you will be whipped for your rudeness.'

'Stand aside,' said Sir Stephen suddenly, 'the bride is coming!'

Then Fair Ellen and her father came riding towards the

church. Fair Ellen had long dark hair and she looked very young and beautiful.

'Why does an old man like you want to marry a beautiful young girl like Fair Ellen?' Robin asked.

'Who is this rude minstrel?' said Sir Stephen, turning to the Bishop. 'How dare he speak to me like this!'

The soldiers moved forwards and took out their swords. Robin pulled his horn from his belt and blew it three times. Suddenly, eighteen outlaws appeared. The outlaws all carried bows and arrows. The soldiers stopped and looked around at Sir Stephen. Then Robin spoke.

'I am sorry, but Fair Ellen cannot marry this old knight,' he said to the Bishop. 'Fair Ellen is already engaged to Allan a Dale.'

At that moment, Allan a Dale stepped forward. He bowed to Ellen and her father.

Sir Stephen was very angry.

'*You* must choose,' he said to Ellen's father. 'Do you wish your daughter to marry a knight, or an outlaw?'

'My daughter must marry a knight,' replied Ellen's father. 'She will marry you, Sir Stephen, as we agreed.'

But then Ellen spoke. 'No Father,' she said. 'I want to marry Allan a Dale. He is the man I love – not Sir Stephen.'

'Be silent daughter,' said her father. 'You know why you have to marry Sir Stephen – I owe him two hundred crowns.'

Robin called to Little John.

'Bring the money for Sir Stephen,' he said.

Little John walked up to Robin and Sir Stephen. In his hands he held two money bags.

'In these bags are two hundred crowns,' Robin told Sir Stephen. 'Please take them so that Ellen can be free to marry who she wants.'

Sir Stephen looked at Robin for a moment, then he reached out and took the money.

'I will not argue with outlaws,' he said to Allan a Dale. 'I have my money so you can keep the girl.'

Then Sir Stephen turned his horse and rode away. His soldiers followed him.

Robin turned to the Bishop.

'Now,' said Robin, 'Allan a Dale must marry Fair Ellen. Will you marry them, my lord Bishop?'

'Who are you?' asked the Bishop.

'I am Robin Hood of Sherwood Forest,' replied Robin.

'God save us from evil,' said the Bishop. 'I will not marry an outlaw.'

'Then Friar Tuck can marry Fair Ellen and Allan a Dale,'

said Robin, 'and afterwards we will all go to the forest for a wedding feast.'

And so Friar Tuck married Allan a Dale and Fair Ellen in the church at Rotherdale. And afterwards they all returned to the forest for a great feast.

'My lord Bishop will be our special guest,' said Robin.

The Bishop of Hereford knew he had no choice, he had to go into the forest with Friar Tuck and the outlaws. But soon even the Bishop was having a good time. Both he and Friar Tuck loved good food and ale, and there was plenty to eat and drink. The Bishop drank so much ale that he started dancing and singing for Robin and the other outlaws. Then he fell into a very deep sleep.

When the Bishop of Hereford left the next morning, his purse did not go with him. Robin Hood had taken all his money.

14

Sir Richard of Lea

It was a bright afternoon in September. Robin Hood and the outlaws were collecting food and wood in the forest when they saw a knight riding a grey horse along the forest path. The knight's face was sad and he was staring down at the ground.

'It looks like we have a guest for supper,' said Robin. 'I will speak to him.'

So Robin stepped into the path. He put up his hand and stopped the knight.

'Stop, good knight,' he said. 'Please will you join us for supper?'

The knight looked at Robin. His eyes were sad, but he tried to smile. 'Who are you and why do you stop a knight on the road?' he asked.

'I am Robin Hood,' said Robin. 'Have you heard of me?'

'I have heard of you,' answered the knight. 'I have also heard that your guests must pay for their supper.'

'That is true, Sir knight,' said Robin. 'But we never take more than our guests have to give.'

'Well, I have nothing to give,' said the knight, 'so I will be a very poor guest at your supper. Let me pass.'

'You speak like a true and gentle knight,' said Robin. 'Please join us this evening. If you tell us your story, that will be enough.'

And so the knight joined the outlaws for supper.

'My name is Sir Richard of Lea,' he told them as he ate. 'My castle and my lands have been pawned[43] to the Abbot of

St Mary's. My son is fighting with King Richard in Palestine. I borrowed money from the Abbot to help my son and the King. The debt is due tomorrow and I cannot pay it. So my castle and my lands will soon belong to the Abbot.'

'How much do you owe the Abbot of St Mary's?' asked Robin.

'I owe him four hundred crowns,' replied Sir Richard.

'Perhaps we can help you,' said Robin. 'The Bishop of Hereford has just left us a little gift. I think we should use that gift to help a good knight.'

The next day, the Sheriff of Nottingham and Sir Guy of Gisbourne went to see the Abbot of St Mary's. Sir Guy of Gisbourne was Prince John's special tax collector. He was a hard man with a dark face and a deep voice.

The men sat down at a long table in the hall of the Abbey of St Mary's. They looked at some papers on the table in front of them.

'The castle and lands of Sir Richard of Lea are very valuable,' Guy of Gisbourne told the Abbot. 'Prince John will be pleased to take them from you.'

'I am happy for him to have them,' replied the Abbot. 'But first I want my money.'

'The Prince is a generous man,' said Sir Guy of Gisbourne. 'He will pay you well for Richard of Lea's castle and land. You will get your money as soon as you sign the papers.'

'What is the time?' asked the Abbot. 'Sir Richard has until noon to pay me four hundred crowns. I cannot sign the papers until then.'

'It is almost noon,' said Sir Guy, 'and we all know that Sir Richard of Lea cannot pay – my tax collectors have been busy. So why wait until noon? Please, sign the papers now.'

'No,' said the Sheriff of Nottingham. 'The Abbot is right. We must wait for half an hour. Sir Richard of Lea is a friend of King Richard, so we must be careful.'

'Bah!' said Sir Guy to the Sheriff. 'When Prince John is King John he will remember his friends, you can be sure. Are you his friend? Or are you a friend of King Richard? *Where is* King Richard? No one knows. Will he ever come home?'

At that moment, the three men heard the sound of horses approaching the abbey. The Sheriff looked out of the window and saw Sir Richard of Lea. There was a servant riding with him.

A few minutes later, Sir Richard and his servant entered the hall. The servant wore a hood and he kept his eyes on the floor.

'Have you brought my money?' asked the Abbot.

'Good Abbot, I am not carrying any money,' said Sir Richard.

'Then your castle and your lands will be mine,' the Abbot replied.

'Will you really leave me with nothing?' asked Sir Richard. 'I am a knight and a true servant of the King.'

'I will be generous,' said the Abbot. 'If you pay me *three* hundred crowns, the castle and lands will be yours.'

Sir Guy of Gisbourne laughed a cruel laugh. 'This knight hasn't got any money,' he said. 'Three hundred crowns, or three crowns – it makes no difference. He cannot pay his debt and his castle and lands shall belong to Prince John.'

Sir Richard looked at Sir Guy with a look of cold anger.

'I do not carry any money,' he said, 'because my servant is carrying it. Did you say *three* hundred crowns? Very well, I shall pay you three hundred crowns – no more and no less.'

The servant came forward. He took four bags of money

63

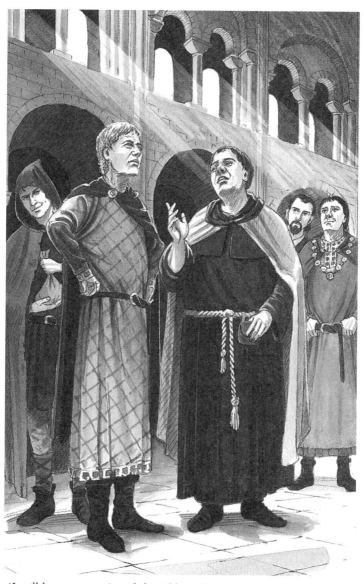

'I will be generous,' said the Abbot. 'If you pay me three hundred crowns, the castle and lands will be yours.'

from under his cloak. He opened three of the bags and poured three hundred gold crowns onto the table.

The Sheriff of Nottingham was staring at the servant. He could not see his face clearly because the servant's head was covered with a hood.

'Have I seen you before?' asked the Sheriff. But the servant did not answer.

'You have your money,' said Sir Richard of Lea. 'And I have my castle and lands back. Now, give me the papers.'

Then Sir Richard of Lea took the papers and walked out of the hall. His servant followed him.

The Abbot, the Sheriff and Sir Guy of Gisbourne were silent. They felt angry and surprised.

'I have lost one hundred crowns,' said the Abbot at last.

'And Prince John has lost a castle and lands,' said Sir Guy. But the Sheriff was thoughtful.

'That servant reminded me of someone,' he said. 'He reminded me of the beggar at the archery contest. I think that servant was Robin Hood!'

———

When they were outside the abbey, Sir Richard said goodbye to Robin.

'I shall tell King Richard about you, Robin Hood,' Sir Richard said. 'I shall tell him how you helped a knight who was in trouble. And I shall tell him how Prince John takes taxes from the ordinary people to make himself rich. When King Richard hears my news, I am sure that he will return to England. He will bring justice to this land at last.'

15

The Black Knight

Sir Guy of Gisbourne and the Sheriff of Nottingham decided to ask Prince John for his help.

'We must catch these outlaws of Sherwood Forest,' Sir Guy told Prince John. 'We must kill Robin Hood.'

Prince John agreed. 'Robin of Locksley has been a problem for too long,' he said. 'We must send an army into Sherwood Forest. A hundred outlaws cannot win against a thousand soldiers.'

The three men made preparations for the battle all winter. They ordered soldiers to Nottingham and collected weapons. They sent men into the forest to find out where Robin and the outlaws were hiding.

Then, on the first day of spring, Sir Guy, the Sheriff and Prince John sent a thousand soldiers into the forest. Finally, they were ready. It was time to attack Robin Hood.

————

That night, Robin dreamed a terrible dream.

'I dreamed that I fought with two strong foresters,' he told Little John. 'They took away my sword and my bow. They tied my hands and feet. One of the foresters was dressed very strangely. He looked like an animal.'

'Dreams do not tell the future,' said Little John. 'We are awake. We know that there are many of the Sheriff's men in the forest around us, they are everywhere. Today, we must fight them. This is no dream.'

'It is the first day of spring today,' said Robin, 'and the White Lady of the Woods has not sung.'

'Stop worrying about the White Lady,' said Little John. 'Forget about dreams and songs. You need to think about the Sheriff. He is planning to catch us here in our camp.'

'We have to find a way out of the forest,' said Robin. 'You go north and I'll go south. Tell the other men that they must find their own way out.'

And so Little John took two outlaws with him and started walking to the north. Robin travelled with Will Scarlett to the south.

After a short time, Little John and the two outlaws reached a clearing. Suddenly a net fell onto Little John. Then ten soldiers jumped down from the trees and tied his hands and feet. The other two outlaws were taken away and Little John did not see them again.

Robin had only travelled a little way when he saw a strange forester. The forester was wearing a coat that was made from animals' tails. His head was covered with a dark hood and he carried a bow and arrow in his hands.

'That man is one of the foresters in my dream,' Robin told Will Scarlett.

Then Will Scarlett stepped forward. 'Who are you and what do you want?' he asked the stranger.

'I am looking for Robin Hood,' said the man in the strange clothes.

'I am Robin Hood,' said Will Scarlett. 'What do you want from me?'

'Your life,' said the man. Suddenly he drew his bow and shot Will Scarlett through the heart.

Immediately Robin took hold of his sword and ran at the forester. But the stranger was quick. He pulled out his sword and began to fight. Then the man pulled back his hood and Robin saw the face of Sir Guy of Gisbourne.

'I am your death!' shouted Sir Guy.

Robin stepped backwards. Then his foot caught something on the ground and he fell. Sir Guy ran forwards, his sword held high. He tried to hit Robin's head but Robin rolled out of the way and Sir Guy's sword hit a tree.

Immediately Robin jumped up and swung his sword at Sir Guy. It hit Sir Guy in the throat and blood ran over his strange coat. Robin swung his sword again. This time he cut off Sir Guy's head.

Now there were two dead men on the ground. One was Sir Guy of Gisbourne. The other was Will Scarlett.

The sound of horns came through the wood. The Sheriff's men were all around the camp. There were terrible sounds of fighting. Swords clashed and men cried out in anger and in pain.

Robin knew he had to get back into the camp and help the other outlaws. Quickly, he took the coat from Sir Guy of Gisbourne's body and put it on. He covered his head with the hood. Then he picked up Sir Guy of Gisbourne's head and carried it towards the sound of fighting.

The Sheriff of Nottingham was the first person to see him coming.

'Look!' the Sheriff cried. 'It is Sir Guy of Gisbourne. He is carrying the head of Robin Hood!'

The fighting stopped for a moment. Everyone looked at the man in the strange coat. The coat was covered with blood and the man's face was hidden as he held up the head.

'See the head of Robin Hood!' the man shouted in a deep voice.

'We also have *this* man,' said the Sheriff. He pointed at Little John. 'We shall hang him from a tree as soon as the fighting is finished.'

'Give him to me,' Robin said in a deep voice. 'I want to kill him now.'

Then Robin took out his sword and walked towards Little John. Little John's hands and feet were tied with ropes. He looked very frightened.

Robin cut Little John's ropes with his sword.

'Stop! What are you doing?' demanded the Sheriff.

Then Robin threw the head to the Sheriff. It hit the ground at the Sheriff's feet.

'This isn't Robin Hood,' shouted the Sheriff. 'This is the head of Sir Guy of Gisbourne!'

Then, before anyone could stop them, Robin and Little John ran through the trees towards the outlaws' camp.

'They cannot escape!' shouted the Sheriff to his men. 'Go after them! Attack from all sides! Kill them all!'

As the Sheriff's men pressed closer, Robin and Little John stood with their backs to the old oak tree. The Sheriff's men were winning the fight. There were too many of them and there were not enough outlaws. Suddenly Will Stutely fell at Robin's feet. He had been hit by a soldier's sword. Many other outlaws were falling and dying in the clearing.

Friar Tuck stood next to Robin and Much the Miller's Son stood beside Little John. Allan a Dale tried to help the wounded[44] and dying men.

Suddenly Robin took out his horn and blew it. The sound of the horn was high and clear. It was like the high note of a song. The wind moved with the sound.

Everybody stopped fighting.

At the other end of the clearing, a strange knight had entered. He was dressed in black and he rode a black horse. The black knight looked down at the Sheriff of Nottingham.

'So many men against so few?' the black knight asked.

'What is the meaning of this, Sheriff?'

The Sheriff of Nottingham's face turned pale as he knelt[45] down before the knight.

'My Lord,' he said, 'we are trying to kill the outlaws.'

'I shall decide who is an outlaw and who is not,' said the black knight. 'Now, stop fighting.'

All the soldiers dropped their swords and dropped onto their knees. The black knight was King Richard. He had returned to England at last.

———

King Richard rode towards the man in the strange coat.

'What is your name?' the King asked.

'My name is Robin Hood, Sir,' Robin replied, and bowed.

'Sir Richard of Lea has told me about you, Robin Hood,' the King said. 'I am going to let you and your men go. You are all free to return to your towns and villages. You, Robin Hood, will become a knight, like your grandfather. Your family's lands will be returned to you. You shall be called Sir Robin of Locksley.'

Robin returned to the town of Locksley. Sadly, Robin's father had died while his son was in Sherwood Forest. Robin now owned his father's farm and lands.

But Maid Marian was still in Locksley, and she had not married. She still loved Robin and she had always been sure that he would return one day.

Robin married Maid Marian and they lived together happily. Little John stayed with them and worked with Robin on the farm. Much the Miller's Son went back to his father's mill and Friar Tuck travelled around the country telling stories about Robin Hood. Allan a Dale and Fair Ellen travelled the country. They sang songs about the brave outlaw.

The black knight was King Richard. He had returned to England at last.

———

The return of King Richard changed many things in England. Richard stopped the Sheriff of Nottingham from collecting taxes. He also stopped the barons and bishops from taking land that did not belong to them.

For a time, England became a place of peace and wealth.

Points for Understanding

1

1 Why did young men practice archery?
2 What could archers win at an archery contest?
3 Why did archers come to Nottingham from all over England?
4 Robin could hit a target from a long distance away. How far away?
5 Why didn't Robin's father want him to go to Nottingham?

2

1 What were the Forest Laws?
2 What did the foresters protect?
3 Why did the foresters laugh at Robin?
4 What was the punishment for killing a deer?
5 Why couldn't the foresters catch Robin?
6 Why was the Sheriff of Nottingham angry?
7 How did the Sheriff learn the name of Robin Hood?

3

1 Who was the first man to join Robin?
2 Why did other men live in the forest?
3 What did the outlaws eat in the forest?
4 What weapons did the outlaws have?
5 Why did the outlaws move every day?
6 Why did Robin decide to make the clearing his permanent camp?
7 What did Robin do with the horn that he found in the old oak tree?

4

1 Why was it easy to guard the camp?
2 What news did Robin want his men to learn?
3 Why was it difficult to cross the river?
4 Why did Robin put down his bow and fight with a quarter-staff?
5 How did Robin show John Little that he was Robin Hood?
6 Why did Robin change John Little's name to Little John?

5

1 What was the Abbot of St Mary's bringing to Nottingham?
2 Why did the knights want to shave their heads?
3 What language did the knights speak?
4 Why did the Abbot of St Mary's dress as a miller?
5 Who walked and rode beside the Abbot when he went into the forest in an open cart?

6

1 What or who was in the covered wagon?
2 Why did the Abbot travel in an open cart followed by women and a child?
3 How did the knights and the Sheriff plan to catch the outlaws?
4 Why did the tall man shout: 'Run! There are too many of them!'?
5 Robin asked: 'Who is the *real* thief here?' What is the answer to this question?
6 Why was Prince John already becoming fat?
7 Why does the Prince say to the Sheriff: 'I think you are a man like myself.'?

7

1 Why did the Sheriff of Nottingham organize an archery contest?
2 What was the name for the black centre of the target?
3 What did the strange beggar look like?

4 Why did the crowd laugh at the beggar?
5 Why was the Sheriff interested in William of London?
6 Why did the Sheriff call the beggar rude?

8

1 Why did the outlaws wear coats of Lincoln green?
2 What news did Robin want from the landlord of the Blue Boar Inn?
3 Why did Will Stutely go into the corner and pray?
4 How did the Sheriff's men recognize Will Stutely as an outlaw?
5 Why did the outlaws and the people press close against the cart?

9

1 Why did Will Scarlett want to join Robin?
2 Why did Robin change Will Gamwell's name to Will Scarlett? Use your dictionary if necessary.

10

1 Why was Much's father hanged?
2 How did Robin know that Much was a strong man?
3 What did Much say that made Robin laugh? Why was it funny?
4 Why does Much say, 'Look in my sack and you will see only flour.'?

11

1 Why was Allan a Dale singing a sad song?
2 What was a minstrel?
3 What story did Allan a Dale tell the outlaws?

12

1 Why did Robin look for Friar Tuck?
2 Friar Tuck wore a sword. Why is this unusual for a religious man?
3 Why did Robin become angry with Friar Tuck?
4 Why did Friar Tuck become angry with Robin?

13

1 When Sir Stephen married Fair Ellen, he would forget her father's debt. What did this mean?
2 Was Sir Stephen more interested in marriage or money?
3 Who married Allan a Dale and Fair Ellen?
4 What did the Bishop of Hereford do at the feast?
5 What did Robin do to the Bishop after the feast?

14

1 Why did Robin invite the knight to supper?
2 'I will be a poor guest at your supper.' The word 'poor' has two meanings here. Can you explain the two meanings?
3 Sir Guy of Gisbourn says, 'Sir Richard of Lea cannot pay.' How does Sir Guy know this?
4 'I am not carrying any money,' said Sir Richard. What did the Abbot and Sir Guy of Gisbourn think Sir Richard meant?
5 Why did Sir Guy of Gisbourn laugh a cruel laugh?

15

1 Why did Will Scarlett say to Sir Guy of Gisbourn, 'I am Robin Hood'?
2 How did Robin disguise himself?
3 How did Robin free Little John?
4 Which words and actions tell us that the Sheriff recognizes King Richard?
5 King Richard pardoned the outlaws. What does this mean?

Glossary

1 **outlaw** (page 4)
   a criminal, especially one who moves from place to place to avoid being caught.

2 **Sheriff** (page 4)
   in Robin Hood's time, the Sheriff was the King's or Queen's representative in a county.

3 **invaded** – *to invade* (page 4)
   to send an army into another country to take control of it.

4 **common** (page 4)
   ordinary, with no special status or rank.

5 **deer** (page 5)
   a large brown animal with long thin legs.

6 **baron** (page 5)
   a powerful man. The King gave land and titles to his best knights and they became barons.

7 **archer** (page 5)
   someone who shoots arrows from a bow.

8 **knight** (page 9)
   a man of high social class who wore armour and carried a sword. He fought for the King.

9 **contest** (page 9)
   a competition where people's skill or talent is tested.

10 **crown** (page 10)
   a coin from a money system used in the past in the UK and some other countries. There were eight half crowns in a pound.

11 **compete** – *to compete* (page 10)
   to try to win a competition.

12 **target** (page 10)
   an object that you have to hit in a game or sport.

13 **paces** (page 10)
   a way of measuring distance. A *pace* is the length of a single step when you walk.

14 **clearing** (page 13)
   an area in a forest where there are no trees or bushes.

15 **ale** (page 13)
   an old word for beer.

16 **aim** – *to aim* (page 14)
   to point a gun or another object at something you want to hit.

17 **realize** – *to realize* (page 17)
   to know and understand something.

18 **barber** (page 17)
   a man who cuts hair and shaves men's faces.

19 **shield** (page 18)
   an object that soldiers carried in the past to protect themselves from being hit by arrows and other weapons.

20 **slope** (page 19)
   a straight surface that has one end higher than the other.

21 **horn** (page 19)
   from the head of a bull. If you blow through a horn it makes a noise.

22 **broad** (page 20)
   wide.

23 **ox** (page 23)
   a large type of cow used on farms for pulling or carrying things.

24 **abbot** (page 24)
   a powerful churchman who is in charge of a religious house called an abbey.

25 **razor** (page 25)
   a small tool or piece of electrical equipment used for *shaving* (= removing hair from your skin).

26 **monk** (page 25)
   a religious man who lived in a religious house called a *monastery* or *abbey*.

27 **abbey** (page 25)
   a large church with buildings connected to it.

28 **whipped** – *to whip* (page 25)
   a long thin piece of leather used to hit men and horses.

29 **miller** (page 27)
   someone who owns or works in a mill where grain is made into flour.

30 **surrounded** – *to surround* (page 28)
   to be all around or on all sides of someone or something.

31 **bowed** – *to bow* (page 32)
   to bend your body forwards from the waist, especially to show respect for someone.

32 **justice** (page 32)
   treatment of people that is fair and right.

33 **harvest time** (page 33)
Early August – the time when a crop (corn, fruit, etc.) is collected.
34 **disguise** – *to disguise* (page 33)
to make changes in the way someone looks so that other people will not recognize them.
35 **steward** (page 34)
someone who helps to organize people at an event.
36 **hood** (page 34)
the part of a coat or jacket that covers your head.
37 **round** (page 34)
a game or a series of games in a competition.
38 **harp** (page 50)
a musical instrument with strings.
39 **minstrel** (page 50)
a travelling musician and singer.
40 **supper** (page 51)
the last main meal of the day, usually an informal meal that you eat at home. It is also called *dinner*.
41 **friar** (page 53)
a travelling priest or religious man.
42 **bishop** (page 57)
a senior priest who is responsible for all the churches in an area.
43 **pawned** – *to pawn* (page 61)
to give something valuable to someone, temporarily, so that you can borrow some money from them.
44 **wounded** – *to wound* (page 69)
hurt or injured.
45 **knelt** – *to kneel* (page 70)
to put one or both knees on the ground.

Dictionary extracts adapted from the Macmillan English Dictionary © Bloomsbury Publishing Plc 2002 and © A & C Black Publishers Ltd 2005.

Exercises

Vocabulary: meanings of words from the story

Put the words and phrases in the box next to the correct meanings.

> disguise   bush   collect   taxes   deer   hollow   hanged
> determined   robber   archery   rule   prize   weapon
> afford   blinded   contest   compete   honest   aim
> steward   wanted   outlaw   hunt   damp   needy
> slope   wagon   miller   common   beggar

1		ordinary; usual; not special
2		money which a government takes from people (the word is plural in the story)
3		to chase and kill animals for food, for their skin or for sport
4		a large brown animal with long thin legs
5		when someone's eyes have been damaged so that they cannot see again
6		killed by putting a rope round someone's neck and making them fall
7		someone who takes money or property from other people illegally
8		(of people) not having enough money for food, clothing or a place to live
9		(of a king) to govern a country
10		the sport of shooting arrows from a bow
11		a reward you get for winning a competition
12		an object such as a sword or a gun that you use to hurt people
13		to have enough money to be able to pay for something

14		a competition – especially a sports competition
15		to try to be more successful than other people in sport or business
16		(of a person) someone who does not tell lies or cheat other people
17		not willing to let anything prevent you from doing something that you have decided to do
18		to point a gun or bow at an object you want to hit
19		(of a person) someone that the police are looking for
20		a plant that is smaller than a tree and has many branches with leaves
21		slightly wet
22		a flat surface that has one end higher than the other
23		empty inside
24		to get money from a person for a particular purpose
25		a vehicle with wheels which is used for carrying heavy loads
26		someone who makes flour from grain
27		something you wear to change the way you look so that other people will not recognize you
28		an old word for a criminal who moves about to avoid being caught
29		an old word for someone whose job was to take care of a house or land; in modern English it can mean a waiter on a plane or ship
30		someone who is very poor and lives by asking people for money and food

Writing: rewrite sentences

Rewrite the sentences using the words and phrases in the box to replace the underlined words.

afford   roast   guard   festival   disguise   ~~poor~~
steal   take care of   minstrel   rude   order
contest   compete   target   common   explore   camp
bull's eye   armour   clearing   barber

Example: Robins' father <u>did not have very much money</u>.
You write: *Robin's father was poor.*

1 Robin's grandfather <u>did not have enough money</u> to pay the Sheriff's high taxes.
Robin's grandfather

2 The King <u>told</u> all young men to practise archery.
The King

3 Every year there were special archery <u>competitions</u>.
Every year

4 Archers came to <u>take part</u> in the contest from all over England.
Archers came

5 Robin came to <u>an open space in the forest</u>.
Robin came

6 'I am a <u>man who cuts hair and shaves beards</u>,' Will Stutely explained to Robin.
'I am a

7 They went to <u>find out about</u> the deepest parts of the forest.
They went

8 The men made <u>a place to stay outdoors</u> in the clearing.
The men

9 'It is not an easy <u>thing to hit</u>,' said Robin.
'It is not

10	I do not love the men who collect taxes from the <u>ordinary</u> people.
	I do not love
11	The outlaws built a great fire and <u>cooked</u> an ox over it.
	The outlaws
12	Knights and soldiers <u>protected</u> the money as he travelled.
	Knights and
13	I am sure that he will try to <u>take</u> the tax money from the Abbot.
	I am sure
14	'My lord, I shall <u>look after</u> it,' said the Sheriff.
	'My lord,
15	There was always a great <u>celebration</u> after the harvest.
	There was
16	'He will try to <u>change his appearance</u>, but we will know him.'
	'He will try
17	But underneath his clothes he was wearing <u>metal clothing for protection</u>.
	But underneath
18	They all hit the centre of the <u>black circle in the middle of the target</u>.
	They all hit
19	'I am a poor <u>wandering singer</u>,' said Alan a Dale.
	'I am a
20	'Who is this <u>impolite</u> minstrel?' said Sir Stephen.
	'Who is this

Vocabulary: anagrams

The letters of each word are mixed up. Write the words correctly.
The first one is an example.

	Example: AWLOUT	
	outlaw	an old word for a criminal
1	STROFE	a large area of land covered by trees and other plants growing close together
2	HERCAR	someone who shoots arrows from a bow
3	ELOP	a long thin stick of wood, used for holding or supporting something (this word has other meanings)
4	DROWS	a weapon with a short handle and a long sharp blade
5	HIRFSEF	the King's representative in Nottingham (in modern American English it means a senior police officer in a town)
6	NOBAR	a powerful man who owned land and soldiers
7	EDAVIN	to send an army into another country to take control of it
8	THINGK	a man of high social class who carried a sword
9	MANESHOD	good-looking
10	DEEDIMNERT	not willing to let anything prevent you from doing something that you have decided to do
11	DIESHL	an object that soldiers carried in the past to protect themselves from being hit by arrows and other weapons

12	DUNDERSOUR	to be all around or on all sides of something or someone
13	JUICEST	treatment of people that is fair and right
14	SHAVERT	the time when a crop is collected
15	TOPCRET	to keep someone or something safe from harm
16	EVARB	able to deal with danger or pain without being frightened
17	DEWDOUN	hurt or injured in a fight
18	MANDED	to say in a strong way that you want something
19	LATEYMIMDIE	very quickly and without delay
20	NOREPAIRAPT	the process of making someone or something ready for something
21	DIMNER	to make someone remember something
22	SECTAL	a large strong building, built in the past to protect people from attack
23	MANCOPY	people you like to spend time with
24	POSHIB	a senior priest who is responsible for all the churches in an area
25	RAFRI	a travelling priest

Grammar: syntax

Put the words into the correct order to make sentences.

Example: He beside the edge of a river lives on the forest.
You write: *He lives on the edge of the forest beside a river.*

1 The life had dead tree come back to.

_____

2 How times live like honest men can in these?

_____

3 I can purse you my money, but it has no show in it.

_____

4 He gates his town and the horse of the back turned through rode.

_____

5 He clothes underneath a sword his carried.

_____

6 They show themselves in the clearing and did not to anyone hid.

_____

7 You eat my ale, can drink my meat and roof under my live.

_____

8 He his head held high above the golden arrow.

_____

Vocabulary Choice: words which are related in meaning

Which word is most closely related? Look at the example and circle the word which is closest in meaning to the word in bold.

	Example:			
	straight road	(upright)	clear	crooked

1	**raise**	lift	ruin	charge	flower
2	**prize**	open	reward	debt	hunt
3	**pleased**	thanked	angry	happy	hurt
4	**trumpet**	instrument	weapon	arrow	staff
5	**hood**	boot	trunk	cover	collar
6	**disguise**	mask	clothe	fit	show
7	**trap**	mouse	catch	invade	cat
8	**thief**	miller	friar	steward	robber
9	**chase**	catch	follow	loose	shoot
10	**abbot**	churchman	beside	minstrel	horn

Vocabulary: opposite meanings

Look at the example and circle the word which is closest to the opposite meaning of the word in bold.

	Example:			
	hit go	exit	quit	(miss)

1	**covered**	hidden	open	disguised	hooded
2	**angry**	mad	annoyed	hot	calm
3	**rich**	wealthy	prosperous	heavy	poor
4	**polite**	civil	respectful	admired	rude
5	**protect**	guard	attack	castle	soldier
6	**drunk**	full	empty	sober	bottle
7	**bright**	dull	shiny	intelligent	sunny
8	**stupid**	dark	foolish	clever	dumb

Macmillan Education
4 Crinan Street
London N1 9XW
A division of Macmillan Publishers Limited
Companies and representatives throughout the world

ISBN 978–0–230–03049–7
ISBN 978–1–4050–8723–0 (with CD edition)

This version of *Robin Hood* was retold by Stephen Colbourn for
Macmillan Readers.
Text © Macmillan Publishers Limited 2007
Design and illustration © Macmillan Publishers Limited 2007

This version first published 2007

Illustrated by John Dillow and Martin Sanders
Cover photograph by Getty Images

Printed and bound in Thailand.

with CD edition

2015 2014 2013
14 13 12 11 10

without CD edition

2015 2014 2013
13 12 11 10 9